0
5/90

•••••••••••••••••••••••••••••••

*MEG
AND THE
DISAPPEARING
DIAMONDS*

•••••••••••••••••••••••••••••••

MEG
AND THE
DISAPPEARING
DIAMONDS

ABOUT THIS BOOK

"A nice day in June. A whole day ahead. Anything might happen," said Mr. Wilson.

"Anything!" Meg repeated his words as she pedaled down the tree-lined drive of her home. Almost immediately things did happen. That morning Meg heard that Mrs. Partlow's Holly House had been broken into, and that very afternoon her garden party was ruined by the appearance of Mrs. Glynn and her poodles. Then just when the guests were calm, they found that the Partlow diamonds were missing!

Meg and her friend Kerry Carmody had many questions. What was Kerry's little cousin Cissie doing at Mrs. Partlow's party? Why did Mrs. Glynn decide to give Meg the collar? And most important to Meg, *where was Thunder?*

When you are Margaret Ashley Duncan and can sense a mystery almost before it's begun, and you have a whole day ahead of you, almost anything can happen—and does—in MEG AND THE DISAPPEARING DIAMONDS.

Meg

AND THE DISAPPEARING DIAMONDS

by Holly Beth Walker

illustrated by Cliff Schule
cover illustration by Olindo Giacomini

GOLDEN PRESS
Western Publishing Company, Inc.
Racine, Wisconsin

CONTENTS

700793

1
WHAT'S SO SECRET?

While Meg Duncan read the Tuesday comic strips, she fed muffin scraps to her Siamese cat, Thunder. His rough tongue raked butter from her fingers. His black tail beat the floor while he waited for his next bite.

Mrs. Wilson, the Duncan's housekeeper, sat on Meg's left. Across the breakfast table sat Mr. Wilson. Mr. and Mrs. Wilson were middle-aged and easy to live with. They were as much a part of Meg's family as Dad himself.

Meg glanced up from the paper when Mrs. Wilson said, "You're feeding that cat at the kitchen table, Meg."

"Yes, ma'am." Meg's words slurred in the pleasant southern way. Her dark eyes shone. Each morning Mrs. Wilson said the same words. Each morning Meg gave the same answer.

Thunder was Meg's dearest pal. He made up, a little, for the mother, brothers, and sisters she did not have. Meg's father was one of the men who work in government in Washington, D.C., but live in the "country." When work took Dad away from home, Meg was not lonesome. She had Thunder.

Thunder crossed his blue eyes at Mrs. Wilson. He jumped into Meg's lap. He put front paws on her shoulders. He rubbed black ears against her chin. "Oh, Thunder," she sang, "I *like* mornings!"

Mr. Wilson—a thin, wiry, balding man—put down the sports page. He said, "A nice day in June. A whole day ahead. Anything might happen."

Anything. What a magic word!

Meg tugged at one long, dark braid. She wrapped its curly tip around a finger. She twinkled at Mr. Wilson. "I might—" she said.

14

Mrs. Wilson rattled her paper. She said, "Oh, my, oh, my, that poor Mrs. Partlow!"

Dryly Mr. Wilson said, "Hannah Partlow is about the un-poorest person in Hidden Springs."

"Un-poor?" Meg asked, giggling.

Mrs. Partlow was "First Lady" of the village of Hidden Springs, Virginia. She lived at Holly House. Her oaks and maples had been planted before the Washingtons built Mount Vernon. Up here in horse country, a Partlow was not just *a* Virginian. A Partlow *was* Virginia. That was not poor.

Mrs. Wilson took off her glasses and polished them. She said, "Her house was broken into. That's all. Nothing was taken."

Meg jiggled in her chair. A mystery! No one broke into a house without a reason.

Mr. Wilson rubbed his bald spot. Meg saw that he looked puzzled. He said, "I wonder what they were after. There's a lot of valuable stuff there."

"Oh, my, oh, my, how should I know what a thief would want?" Mrs. Wilson answered.

15

Meg imagined herself a thief. She squinted her dark eyes. She pulled her eyebrows into a straight, dark line. Sounding fierce, she said, *"I'd* take silver and gold and jewels. Lots of 'em!"

Mr. Wilson stuck out a forefinger and raised a thumb. "Bang!" he said. "I got you. Hand over those diamonds!"

Meg fell back in her chair. She held her chest with both hands. She gasped.

Mrs. Wilson mused, "Mrs. Partlow's silver is too old-fashioned to steal. If she has any gold, she keeps it locked up. I wonder—"

Meg bounced to life again. "About what?"

"Your playacting put an idea in my head," Mrs. Wilson said. She shrugged. "Oh, my. It's too silly to think about."

"What? What's silly?" Meg asked.

"Well, it's about jewels. Everyone knows Mrs. Partlow inherited her family's diamonds. Land knows, there's been plenty of talk about her diamonds ever since she took them out of the vault. She's going to wear them to her niece's wedding."

16

"I know that," Meg said impatiently. "She promised to let me see them. Are you *sure* they weren't stolen?"

"I'm sure," Mrs. Wilson answered.

Meg lifted Thunder to her shoulder. She said, "Excuse me."

"Yes, dear," Mrs. Wilson said. "What are you planning to do?"

"Find my ballet slippers," Meg told her. "I let Cissie Carmody try them on, and they disappeared. Every time Kerry and I let Cissie touch our things, whoosh! Away they go!"

Mr. Wilson chuckled. He said, "Kerry's little cousin has pack-rat habits."

"She's very young. She means no harm," Mrs. Wilson said.

As Meg passed Mr. Wilson, Thunder batted a paw. Mr. Wilson glared at Thunder. He said, "That danged wildcat! He'll come to no good end!"

Anxiously Meg bent to look at Mr. Wilson's left ear. With spirit she said, "Thunder was just playing, Mr. Wilson."

18

"If that's play, don't bring him around when he wants to fight," Mr. Wilson grumbled.

Meg stalked across the kitchen. Limp as a rag doll and purring loudly, Thunder let himself be carried. "Never mind, Thunder," Meg said. "I love you."

When she reached the kitchen door, Mr. Wilson called, "Friends, Meg?"

Meg waggled one of Thunder's black paws at Mr. Wilson. "Friends," she said.

Mr. Wilson squinted at the cat. "I dunno. I can see that tiger's claws. He's fixing to make mincemeat of somebody, sure."

"Mincemeat. That reminds me," Mrs. Wilson said. "There's no cat food, Meg."

"Really?" Meg asked in alarm. "I'll bring some from the pet shop. I'll see if Kerry can go to the village with me."

Outside the kitchen door, Meg took her bicycle from its rack. She fitted Thunder into the wire basket. She pedaled past the dining-room windows.

Ivy grew on the fireplace chimney. There, a

bright red cardinal looked for insects. Thunder dived from Meg's basket. He missed the bird.

The cardinal flew into one of the catalpas shading the side lawn. The bird screamed at Thunder. Mrs. Wilson scolded through the kitchen window, "Thunder! Stay away from the birds!"

The cat thumped his black tail. He stalked off to explore the pansy bed.

Down the curving, oak-shaded drive Meg whizzed. She was glad to be alive on a June morning when anything might happen before the day was over.

"Anything," Meg sand. "Anything!"

Eagerly Meg watched for Kerry Carmody, her best friend. At this hour of the day, Kerry would be on a horse. Kerry loved horses as dearly as Meg loved her cat.

Though Meg liked to be out of doors, she chose a paint box instead of a saddle, and ballet slippers instead of boots.

The Duncan and Carmody places were separated by a stream called Cricket Run. Up beyond the Carmody barn, a log bridge crossed the creek. The girls ran across this "meadow bridge" a dozen times a day.

But when Meg rode her bicycle, she went down Culpepper Road. She passed the Partlow mansion. Then she rode up Old Bridge Road and over the stone bridge.

Meg enjoyed the morning coolness on her face. The road curved in and out among houses of brick or white clapboard. Most of the houses had been built before the Revolution. A house less than one hundred years old was new in Hidden Springs.

Dad had found and restored an old two-story house. Meg loved every wall, floor, and window. Most of all, she liked it because it was within easy walking or bicycling distance of the Carmody farm.

Beyond the Partlow grounds, Meg could see rolling grassland enclosed by white fences. In the meadow Kerry rode her brown pony, Chappie. She practiced the figure eight. Meg shouted, but Kerry did not hear her.

From the top of the slope, Meg looked back at Holly House, Mrs. Partlow's home. Its many old chimneys rose among the green leaves of maples and walnuts. "I wonder what that thief wanted," she muttered.

Something moved near Mrs. Partlow's gate. Meg had a lump of curiosity as big as her own imagination, and that was endless. She turned in the road.

Silently Meg coasted back to the gate. There she found Kerry's nine-year-old brother, Mike. His bicycle leaned against an oak. He stared over the hedge. From his actions, Meg knew Mike did not want to be seen. He jumped when he saw her. "Ssh!" he said.

"What's so secret?" Meg asked. "Nothing was stolen. It said so in the paper."

"I know," Mike said. "But the thief might come back. You never can tell." Mike wanted to be a newspaperman. He was always on the lookout for his "big story."

"Yes-s," Meg said. "He might."

Kerry rode across the stone bridge and down the road on her brown pony. She shouted, "Don't do anything till I get there!"

When she reached the hedge, Kerry grinned widely. "Hi, Meg! I suppose you have the mystery solved. You know who went in Mrs. Partlow's house, and why, and you're telling Mike, and he's writing the story, and—"

"And I'm going to the pet shop for Thunder's food," Meg cut in, smiling back at Kerry. "Want to go with me?"

"Sure," Kerry said at once. "Trade you my horse for your bicycle, Mike."

Mike jerked a thumb at his bicycle. Kerry swung down from Chappie's back. She dropped the reins. Chappie began to pull heads from clover.

As the girls pedaled away from Mrs. Partlow's hedge, Meg looked back. Mike had not moved. He was staring at the big front door. She said, "Mike is right. He might."

"Huh?" Kerry asked.

But Meg did not explain.

2
A HINT OF MYSTERY

The pet shop was on the village square, a block from the constable's office. Meg waved to Constable Hosey. As she went through the shop door, a bell tinkled. Mr. Wayburn came from the back room.

Birds sang and twittered in cages. Kerry whistled at a canary. Meg went to the counter to pay for a carton of cat food.

On the counter lay a collar of soft leather. It was trimmed with tiny, shiny bells. "Oh," Meg said. "This would fit Thunder!"

Meg picked up the collar. The bells tinkled pleasantly. She called Kerry. Together the girls looked at the collar.

Meg said, "Don't you just love it, Kerry? If Thunder wore this, the birds would hear him. Then Mrs. Wilson wouldn't scold him."

She turned to Mr. Wayburn. "How much is it? If it's more than I have, I'll pay for it out of my allowance, twenty-five cents a week, and—"

"Hold on, Meg," Mr. Wayburn said. "This collar isn't for sale."

"Not—for—sale?" Meg asked slowly.

"It was made for the wardrobe of some poodles who just moved to the village," Mr. Wayburn explained.

"W-Wardrobes? For dogs?" Kerry giggled so hard that Meg giggled, too. Their laughter set a canary to singing. At once every bird in the room raised an uproar.

"Ssh, ssh," Mr. Wayburn begged. To Meg and Kerry he said, "When that bird sings, I can't hear myself think. I wish somebody would buy him and take him out of here!" He threw a dark cloth over the canary's cage to quiet him.

As he came back to the counter, Mr. Wayburn

26

asked, "Haven't you girls met Mrs. Glynn? She's the one who ordered this collar. It's for one of her poodles."

"No," Kerry said.

"But we'd like to," Meg said eagerly. Mrs. Glynn was an actress from New York who was resting between shows. She had rented a house on Upland Way, not far from Meg's home.

Mr. Wayburn smiled. He rubbed his palms together. He said, "Well, then, you haven't met Enfant, Petite, and Jouet."

Kerry puckered her blond brows. Meg whispered, "Those must be the dogs' names."

"That's right, Meg. They're about the smartest poodles you ever saw," Mr. Wayburn said. "I call them Child, Little One, and Toy. Mrs. Glynn says that's what those fancy French names mean."

"That's easier," Meg said politely. "But what about their wardrobes? Do they wear doll clothes?"

"*Doll* clothes!" Mr. Wayburn whistled. He bent to pull a box from under the counter. "Let me show you some of the outfits we've made for those dogs."

He brought out a gun belt, a holster, and a cowboy hat with a rubber chin band. "These are for Toy," he said.

"Cowboy clothes!" Kerry giggled. She twirled the gun on the tip of a finger. "Meg, wouldn't Cissie have a fit if she saw this? She would want it for Cecil."

Cissie was Kerry's small cousin who was spending the summer on the farm. Cecil was the rag doll she dragged around with her.

Kerry unsnapped the holster. Meg put the gun back in place. Mr. Wayburn showed them Child's pink velvet hair bow and necklace.

"Pret-ty fan-cy," Meg said.

"Child usually wears pink," he said. "But this one takes the cake." He held up a mesh tube fastened by a zipper. He poked his thumbs through two holes to show where the poodle's front legs belonged. The tube was of silver threads. It was covered with sequins, pearls, and shiny glass beads.

To go with the glittering coat, he showed them a crown. He asked, "Can you beat this? This crown has a real diamond set in it. A *real* diamond!"

Meg and Kerry bumped heads in their hurry to look at the crown. It was no bigger than a bracelet for Cissie's wrist.

"Diamonds? For a dog?" Kerry puffed out her cheeks and blinked her blue eyes.

The shop bell tinkled. A cool voice asked, "Do you like it?"

Meg whirled to face a very tall, slender lady with smooth black hair pulled back in a bun. She wore a slim dress. Her red shoes had very high heels. Her red earrings looked so heavy Meg wondered if they stretched her ears.

"Y-Yes, ma'am," Meg said. "It's beautiful."

At the woman's feet pranced three poodles on red leather leashes. One dog was white, one was black, and the third, brown. Perfectly clipped and combed, they sat in a row. Long, sharp noses tilted. Black eyes stared at Meg.

Meg forgot about their owner. She dropped to her knees to look at the pampered dogs. Politely they held up small paws.

"Say 'How do you do,' " the cool voice ordered. They barked, one after the other, like toots from a flute.

Meg shook each paw when it was offered. "Come, look," she urged Kerry. "Their toenails are painted red."

Kerry sat on her heels beside Meg. She blinked her pale eyelashes so hard that Meg asked, "Do you have something in your eye, Kerry?"

"No!" Kerry whispered back. "Look at that lady's eyes. Our best cow doesn't have eyelashes that long."

"They're not real," Meg said.

"Honest?" Kerry asked doubtfully.

"They're fur. She glues them on," Meg explained. "Did you ever see such little dogs? Thunder weighs more than all three together."

"I wonder who clips them," Kerry said.

Each poodle was clipped in a different way. Puffs of fur stood out from patches of shaved skin. The brown dog looked like a toy lion with a long nose. This had to be Toy, owner of the gun belt.

The black poodle seemed to have pushed her

32

head through a fluffy black powder puff. She had patches of fur on her hips and circles of fur around her ankles. Even her tail was shaved, with a black tassel at the tip.

Meg tapped her teeth with a fingertip. She said, "The black dog couldn't wear the silver coat. She has too much fur around her neck. She'd get all tangled up. So," Meg decided, "the white dog must be Petite."

This dog had chest and neck shaved bare. Long ears almost touched the floor. When Meg touched the dog's skin, it felt like a soft kid glove.

"I think you're right," Kerry said. "Child is the black poodle. When she wears a hair ribbon, I'll bet she looks like one of Cissie's stuffed toys."

While the girls played with the poodles, they paid little attention to the woman. Then Meg heard the actress say, "I really can't let you sell that collar, Mr. Wayburn. You know I don't sell my designs."

Meg turned to look at the pair at the counter. Mr. Wayburn said, "Yes, ma'am," and "No, ma'am," at the right places. His face was so red Meg felt

33

sorry for him. She went to the counter for her carton of cat food.

As the girls turned to leave the shop, Meg told Mrs. Glynn, "You'd better keep track of Petite when she wears that crown. There may be a thief around here. Mrs. Partlow's house was broken into last night."

"Thank you for warning me," the tall woman said. She stooped to untangle the three red leashes. She said coolly, "You're right. She might lose it. Yes . . . she might."

As they left the village, Kerry burst out, "My goodness, she pays more attention to those dogs than Ma'am pays to all of us and all our horses."

Ma'am and Sir were Kerry's parents. Kerry had five brothers and a small sister. And so many cousins came and went that Meg lost count. At the moment, Cissie was living at the farm. Meg did not know how many horses the Carmodys owned. She did know life was lively on the Carmody farm, and no living thing was neglected.

They pedaled to the driveway of Meg's house.

Meg asked, "Kerry, have you seen my ballet slippers?"

"Didn't Cissie give them back to you?"

"No."

"Well!" Kerry tossed her red-blond hair. Stormily she said, "We'll have to find her playhouse. She moves it so often I haven't any idea where she's hiding things today."

"Wait for me while I take this cat food to Mrs. Wilson," Meg said. "Then we'll look for Cissie!"

Within a few minutes, the girls were riding around a curve where three winding country roads met. When they reached the Partlow hedge, Mike was still there.

Meg asked, "What's going on, Mike?"

Mike answered, "Nothing. Did you expect the thief to come back in broad daylight?"

"No," Meg said.

"Why are you hanging around if you know nothing is going to happen?" Kerry asked Mike.

"Something *might* happen," Mike argued.

Meg joined Mike and looked over the hedge.

36

A hint of mystery drew Meg as a magnet draws nails. She wanted to see where the thief had entered and what clues he might have left. She had the perfect excuse to go through the gate. Mrs. Partlow had asked her to look at the diamonds.

"Let's go in," Meg told Kerry eagerly.

"What about your slippers?" Kerry asked.

Impatiently Meg said, "We'll hunt for them later. Kerry, the wedding is Friday night. Mrs. Partlow will put the diamonds back in the vault. Then we'll never see them."

"Are you sure it's all right for us to go in?" Kerry hung back. The children of Hidden Springs kept their distance from the owner of Holly House.

"She invited me," Meg said.

Kerry leaned Mike's bike against the oak tree. She followed Meg through the gate.

3

DIAMONDS

A winding shell path led to the side door of Holly House, where even the bricks were pink with age.

Arborvitae was clipped to look like green vases ten feet tall. It grew in long rows under ancient maples and sycamores. Creeping phlox, candytuft, and yellow alyssum grew in the sun. In the shady corners of the garden stood the shiny holly bushes. These gave the place its name.

Kerry tiptoed as she walked.

Meg asked, "Do you have a pebble in your shoe?"

"No," Kerry said with a nervous giggle. "I'm afraid I'll touch something I shouldn't."

Before they reached the door, they found Mrs. Partlow in the garden. A workman stood on a ladder. Mrs. Partlow watched. She called, "Hello, Meg. We are mending the window."

Alertly Meg looked at the ground under the window. It was punched full of holes by the ladder's legs. Some holes were smaller than others. If there had been footprints, they were messed up now.

Meg pulled Kerry forward. She said, "You remember Kerry, Mrs. Partlow."

"Of course. Kerry Carmody. How are you?"

Wide-eyed, Meg and Kerry looked at Mrs. Partlow's ears, throat, fingers, and wrists.

Mrs. Partlow moved her shoulders. She asked, "Have I lost a button?"

"Oh, no, ma'am," Meg said quickly. "We thought you might be wearing your diamonds. . . ."

Mrs. Partlow looked surprised, then amused. "I don't wear them gardening, dear. They are much too valuable to risk losing them out of doors."

"Then they weren't stolen?" Meg asked.

"Thank goodness, no," Mrs. Partlow said. "The

newspaper publicity about the wedding has worried me. It seems to *ask* a thief to come take my diamonds."

She patted a crisp, white handkerchief between her palms. She crumpled it nervously. She added, "The Barbour diamonds have been in my family over two hundred years. My grandmother was a Barbour in tidewater Virginia, you know."

"Yes, ma'am," Meg said. In Hidden Springs, neighbors knew about family trees.

"I want my neighbors to share the beauty of the diamonds," Mrs. Partlow said. "I am asking a number of friends in for tea in the garden this afternoon. Can you come?"

Meg dimpled with pleasure. Kerry's freckled face glowed. "Thank you!" they said happily. "We'll be here."

The minute the girls were outside the hedge, Kerry told Mike, *"We* have been invited to a ruffles and hair-ribbon party, brother, dear."

"By Mrs. Partlow? Honest?" Mike looked impressed, but not for long. He asked Meg, "What did you see? Did you find a clue?"

"Nothing," Meg told him. "We couldn't snoop. It wouldn't have been polite." She added with a smile, "Come, help us find Cissie's playhouse, Mike."

"Sure," Mike said. "But first I'll ride Chappie home. I heard Ma'am ask Bertha to bake gingerbread. I like it hot."

"Mmm, me, too," Meg said.

Kerry begged, "Meet us at the bridge in half an hour and bring some gingerbread. Please, Mike?"

"Okay." Mike mounted Chappie and urged him to a gallop around the curve where the roads met.

Right on time the three met at the stone bridge on Old Bridge Road. They sat on the edge and

dangled their feet while they ate gingerbread.

Meg, Kerry, and Mike spent two hours searching for Cissie's playhouse and Meg's missing ballet slippers. They found clues at the places Cissie had been. A paper doll fluttered in Miss Upshur's grape arbor. One domino lay on Miss Culpepper's brick pavement. A gum wrapper was on the bridge.

"We know where she's been. But where is she now?" Kerry cried.

"Cissie!" Meg muttered.

Later Mrs. Wilson and Meg met Ma'am and Kerry at Mrs. Partlow's hedge gate. At the same time, Mr. Wayburn drove up in his station wagon. He helped Mrs. Wayburn out of the car. Then he ambled off to speak to Mrs. Partlow's gardener. He left the car door open.

Meg caught a glimpse of the things her neighbors had bought today. Mr. Wayburn was delivering a case of dog food to somebody, and a stack of baskets and a birdcage.

Mrs. Wilson, Ma'am, Mrs. Wayburn, Kerry, and Meg walked through the grounds together. Meg admired the matching mother-daughter dresses worn by the blond Carmodys. She told them so.

Kerry said, "I like your dress, too, Meg."

Meg dimpled. She walked with a dancer's grace. She liked the swish of her full-skirted party dress. Even with the long, dark braids she hated, she felt pretty. She liked the feeling.

Meg liked beautiful things. She liked to draw the people, things, and places that pleased her. It excited her, knowing that any minute she would see jewels so beautiful and valuable they must be kept in a vault.

Wearing lavender, Mrs. Partlow walked forward to meet her guests. Meg saw that she did not blaze with diamonds.

"Be patient, dear," Mrs. Partlow said. She patted Meg's shoulder. "I'll bring them out when we have had our cakes and tea."

The garden was bright with flowers, hummingbirds, and butterflies. Mrs. Partlow's Callie served spiced tea in thin cups. She passed a tray of delicious small cakes around.

45

Meg and Kerry sat close together. They listened to the women talk. They watched the neighbors: Miss Upshur, twittery and tiny; Miss Culpepper, dark-skinned and bony; Mrs. Hosey, the constable's wife, plump and smiling; and Mrs. Wayburn, silent and nervous in her movements.

Meg was pleased with the way Mrs. Wilson looked. Her gray hair was not fussily arranged. The blue dress she wore hung in soft folds.

The women talked about their gardens, their dinner menus, and the coming wedding. But they were not much interested in their own talk.

Meg was glad when Miss Upshur twittered, "Hannah, dear, you just know why we're here. We can't bear it another minute, not another minute! We're dying to see those diamonds!"

Mrs. Partlow rose from a wicker basket chair. "You shall see them," she promised as she went into the house.

At that moment, a ball of brown fluff bounced from behind a holly bush. It was followed by a black and then by a white ball of fluff.

"Toy!" Kerry cried. "Why, it's Toy!"

"Enfant and Petite!" Meg added. "Where did you come from?"

"I'm sorry," a cool voice said. Mrs. Glynn walked into the garden party. "I've been chasing these naughty ones down Upland Way. This is where they brought me. I hope you don't mind."

Prettily the actress spread her hands. She lifted long, black lashes. Slowly she turned to look at each person present.

Kerry whispered to Meg, "Isn't she gorgeous? Ma'am doesn't look like that when she chases us."

"Look!" Meg whispered back. "The dogs are wearing their new clothes."

And so they were. Toy strutted in his cowboy outfit. Child posed and fluttered her own long lashes. She rolled her eyes at the big bow on her forehead. Petite shimmered and glittered each time she moved.

"Sit up. Say 'How do you do,' " Mrs. Glynn commanded. At once the trio lined up. They barked in flutelike voices.

"Now say you're sorry you came without being

asked,'' she said. At once the poodles dropped their heads like heavy roses on weak stems. Tears ran down their long, sharp noses.

Mrs. Partlow returned from the house. She carried a blue velvet jewel box, but no one noticed. All eyes were on the dogs.

''Aren't the dogs precious?'' Miss Upshur twittered to Mrs. Partlow. ''Did y'all ever see anything like them in all your born days?''

With a gracious movement of one hand, Mrs. Partlow said, ''Do join us, Miss—?''

''Mrs. Glynn,'' the stranger said. ''I'm one of your new neighbors. I've rented the cottage behind Miss Upshur's orchard. You'll see us often. We walk every day.''

''How—nice,'' Mrs. Partlow said politely.

4

A VERY UNUSUAL PARTY

From the minute she walked across the lawn, Mrs. Glynn took charge of Mrs. Partlow's garden tea. She paraded the circle. One hand held the three red leashes of the prancing poodles. The other made wide gestures.

Mrs. Partlow's guests soon tired of the dog show. They had come to see diamonds, not dogs. But they clapped hands and smiled politely. They tried to ignore the actress. She would not be ignored.

"Sit up!" she ordered her dogs. "Roll! Dead dog!" There was no end to their tricks.

Mrs. Partlow fanned her face with her handkerchief. The guests moved restlessly.

"The diamonds, Hannah, please, dear?" Miss Upshur twittered at last.

"Oh, yes, the diamonds," Mrs. Hosey said.

But Mrs. Glynn announced, "My precious pets will race for you." They raced in circles, ears flapping, tails bouncing.

"Oh, my, oh, my," Mrs. Wilson said, not too quietly. "Doesn't that woman know when to sit down and keep quiet?"

Only Mrs. Wayburn clapped for the dogs. At last even she stopped.

Mrs. Partlow opened the jewel box. Sunlight hit the diamonds lying in their blue velvet nest. "Oh-h," sighed the guests.

Mrs. Glynn bent over Mrs. Partlow's chair. Meg and Kerry moved closer, hoping to see the diamonds. Mrs. Glynn blocked their view.

In shocked surprise the actress said, "Mrs. Partlow, those can't be real!" She called loudly, "Come over here, everyone!"

Meg and Kerry joined the guests who crowded around Mrs. Partlow.

"The necklace," Mrs. Partlow said. She held up a spider-web mesh of platinum and diamonds. "The bracelet. The earrings. And the snood."

"Oh-h," Meg breathed.

Kerry whispered, "What's a snood?"

"It covers the hair on the back of your head," Meg whispered back.

Miss Upshur twittered, "Do you mind, dear? May I—just touch them, Hannah?"

"Of course, dear," Mrs. Partlow said.

The guests took turns trying on the diamonds. Mrs. Glynn was first to put on the bracelet. She tossed it to Ma'am. Kerry's mother was so startled she almost dropped it.

Kerry grabbed Meg's hand. She did not turn it loose until the bracelet was on Miss Upshur's wrist. Then she burst out, "The way that Mrs. Glynn throws diamonds around, she must own a bushel!"

"She's just plain rude," Meg answered. Her words were so sharp that even her drawl disappeared.

Meg noticed that Mrs. Glynn looked longer at the necklace. Then suddenly the poodles began their wild race. In and out they ran, dragging leashes, tangling neighbor with neighbor.

Meg wanted to try on the necklace, but she lost track of it while Mrs. Glynn chased Petite. At last the actress caught the racing dog. She patted the shining coat. "Naughty girl, go sit in a corner," she said.

At once Petite walked on her spindly hind legs. Her glittering coat flashed as she went through a patch of sunlight. Then she sat by a holly bush, motionless as a china dog.

Meg looked at the diamond-studded snood. She passed it to Mrs. Glynn. Miss Upshur waited her turn.

Toy began to bounce like a jumping jack. Mrs. Glynn, too, bounced on her high heels till she laid her hands on Toy.

She scooped him up in her lap and adjusted his cowboy hat. She even opened his holster and took out the small gun. Then she talked baby talk while she pretended to snap the gun. The dog barked.

"Please?" Miss Upshur twittered.

Mrs. Glynn hugged Toy. She ordered, "Go join your sister!" Away ran Toy to sit by the holly bush with Petite.

Meg felt sorry for Mrs. Partlow, whose party was being ruined.

With a nervous giggle, Mrs. Wayburn offered to show Mrs. Glynn the earrings. Mrs. Glynn smoothed her black hair and patted the bun. She moved a hairpin while she dangled an earring out where the sun would hit the large diamond.

Mrs. Glynn was standing beside the tea table.

Suddenly she tripped. Both hands went into the tray of cakes as she kept herself from falling. She held up icing-smeared hands. "Oh, I'm so sorry!" she cried. Snatching Child's red leash, she limped across the lawn to Toy and Petite. She took her dogs down the shell path.

Quiet fell on the little group. Miss Upshur put the blue velvet box into Mrs. Partlow's hands. Shakily she said, "T-Take your d-diamonds, Hannah, before anything else happens. You know we're sorry about what happened, dear."

Mrs. Partlow fanned her face with her handkerchief. She said loudly and clearly, "People say I give unusual parties. In my opinion, this one is unique."

Kerry raised her blond eyebrows at Meg.

"Nothing like it," Meg explained.

"Boy, she can say that again!" Kerry said.

Callie came forward to take the blue box from Mrs. Partlow. Mrs. Partlow lifted the lid.

"What—?" she gasped. "Where—?"

"Hannah, dear, what is it?" cried Miss Upshur. She ran toward her hostess.

"There—is nothing here—but the bracelet," Mrs. Partlow said. Her face turned white, then reddened.

"Miz Hannah, honey, you've been robbed," Callie shouted.

Ma'am Carmody said soothingly, "Let's not get excited. Someone has the jewels. She will put them back."

Neighbor looked at neighbor. Not one person stepped forward. Meg gulped.

"I feel like a thief," Kerry whispered.

"Me, too," Meg said. Meg loved a mystery. But now that she found herself in the middle of one, she could only stare at Mrs. Partlow's worried face.

"Let's search the place," Mrs. Wilson said. Ma'am Carmody agreed with her.

Busily the worried guests searched chairs and table, trays and cups, even their own purses. Ma'am and Mrs. Wilson dropped to their knees to help Meg and Kerry hunt through grass.

Mrs. Glynn came back. She cried happily, "How did you know I'd lost it?"

"Lost what?" Kerry asked.

"Toy's gun," Mrs. Glynn said. "I must have dropped it." She too, crawled on her knees. She patted the lawn around the chair where she had sat when not chasing or showing off her dogs.

Miss Culpepper boomed in her big voice, "I found that silly gun. It isn't important. Hannah's diamonds are missing!"

"Oh, no!" Mrs. Glynn cried. "They can't be missing!"

"Oh, but they are!" Miss Upshur wailed.

Mrs. Glynn studied Ma'am's face. "You *do* mean it," she said. She put palms against cheeks while she thought. Suddenly she cried, "The cakes! Have you searched the table?"

Ma'am Carmody was nearest the table. She reached for the tray. Meg and Kerry reached the table just in time to see Mrs. Glynn lift something from a mashed teacake.

"An earring!" Meg said gladly.

Mrs. Partlow took the earring and held it in cupped hands.

"It's covered with icing," Kerry said.

"It can be washed," Mrs. Partlow said.

Nothing else was found. The snood, necklace, and one earring were missing.

Mrs. Glynn walked to Mrs. Partlow. She said, "This is my fault. My dogs caused the fuss. I insist that you search me."

"Really, Mrs. Glynn," Mrs. Partlow said.

"She's right, Hannah," Miss Culpepper boomed. "We must all be searched."

Soberly the women searched each other. Not a sparkle was found. Silently they went home. Silently Mrs. Partlow watched them go.

Meg and Kerry walked together. As they passed a holly bush, Meg saw something move. "Cissie!" she gasped.

"What are you doing?" Kerry asked.

Wide-eyed and angelic-looking, the small girl combed fingers through silky, long blond hair. Sweetly she piped, "I'm being at a party." Sadly she said, "Nobody asked me. I just comed by myself."

Kerry frowned. She asked, "How long have you been here, Cissie Carmody?"

"Are you thinking what I think you're thinking, Kerry?" Meg asked.

"What else?" Kerry said. "Everything Cissie touches disappears. Mrs. Partlow's diamonds are gone. Here is Cissie."

Cissie backed into a holly bush. Kerry followed. She shouted, "You've been eating cake, Cissie. You have crumbs on your face! One earring was in the cake. *Where* is that other earring, Cissie Carmody?"

"You go 'way!" Cissie ordered. But Kerry did not go away. She grabbed Cissie's arms.

"Don't touch me, Kerry," Cissie warned. "Ma'am says no kicking, no biting, no—"

Kerry said hotly, "Ma'am didn't say anything about shaking! I'm going to shake you till that earring rattles right out of your teeth!"

"I'll tell Sir!" Cissie wailed.

Kerry made angry fists of her hands, but she backed away. She said, "Meg, Cissie has had plenty of time to hide the earring and all out-of-doors to hide it in."

Cissie ran.

5
FOOTPRINTS

Cissie ran from Mrs. Partlow's garden and onto Old Bridge Road. Kerry followed. Angrily she shouted, "Wait till I get my hands on you, Cissie, I'll—I'll—"

Meg ran one step behind Kerry. She cried, "Hush, Kerry. People will hear you." Meg looked back at the guests leaving the garden. She saw a car swing into the driveway. There was a star on the door. "Kerry!" Meg warned. "Here comes Constable Hosey."

"What of it?" Kerry yelled. Then she stopped so suddenly that Meg ran into her. "Police?" Kerry croaked. "Oh, Meg, we can't let the police catch

Cissie.'' Kerry's anger turned to fear for Cissie's safety.

There, in the middle of the road, Meg put her arms around Kerry. She talked to herself as much as to Kerry.

She said, ''Nobody knows Cissie was at the party. The constable will talk to the grown-ups. We'll hunt for Cissie's hiding place. When we find the earring, we'll tell Cissie it isn't a toy. Then Cissie will take it back, and no one will think she's a thief.''

''A THIEF? CISSIE? Oh-h!'' Kerry cried.

''Sssh, ssh,'' Meg whispered.

Meg watched Cissie cross Old Stone Bridge. Then she said, ''There. Cissie is almost home. I'm sure no one saw her. Let's go back to see if she really went to that table.''

At the holly bush, Kerry said, ''Cissie must have crawled through the flower beds.''

''She's little,'' Meg said. ''No one would have noticed. The dogs were acting up.''

Meg was first to find a small sandal print. Cissie had gone to the table where the earring was last

seen. Also, Cissie had moved a number of times. At some time she had sat very close to Mrs. Partlow's basket chair. That meant she had been very close to *all* of the missing diamonds.

Kerry said grimly, "We know what happens to things when Cissie gets close to them."

"We know she *could* have taken them. She was here," Meg said soberly. "So were we."

Kerry blinked back tears, then walked away when a bell rang. That bell was the signal for all Carmodys, big and little, to return to the farm.

Soberly Meg walked across the tree-shaded grass between the Duncan and Partlow houses. Right across the creek lay the Carmody farm. Now that the diamonds were missing, trouble would come. Some very dear people would be hurt.

Mrs. Wilson served the evening meal on the patio. She talked of nothing but diamonds. "Stolen! That's what they were. Right from under our very noses."

"No proof," Mr. Wilson said mildly.

"Then where are they? Show them to me."

"How should I know?" The man shrugged and

spread his hands. "They may turn up in some unlikely spot."

Yes, Meg thought. *In Cissie's playhouse, I hope. But where is that? Will we find it before Constable Hosey finds her footprints?*

"Oh!" Meg gasped. "Excuse me," she said hurriedly. "I must call Kerry."

At the telephone, Meg whispered, "Kerry, there's something we must do. Meet me at the holly bush in ten minutes."

"I haven't had dessert," Kerry wailed.

"Share mine," Meg said. "Remember, it's for Cissie."

"Okay," Kerry agreed.

Both girls reached the holly bush at the same time. "W-Well?" Kerry panted.

"We can't let the police find Cissie's footprints," Meg said. "We must rub them out."

It was almost dark when the girls patted out the last footprint in the soft dirt of the flower beds. They crossed the grass to the Duncan patio and shared Meg's lemon pie.

"Hope you caught that mole," Mr. Wilson said dryly.

"What mole?" Meg asked in surprise.

"The one you've been digging for," the man said. He raised thick eyebrows.

Meg and Kerry traded a long look. They went upstairs to Meg's bathroom. While they washed hands and bare legs, they listened to a radio report.

The local announcer said, "Unless the missing Partlow diamonds are found tonight, outside help will be called in on the case."

Silently the girls went downstairs again. Mrs. Wilson called from the kitchen, "You have company, Meg. Out on the patio." She clattered the pan she was washing.

Meg frowned. It was not like Mrs. Wilson to walk off and leave a guest alone.

The girls stepped into the dim light of the patio. A black powder puff seemed to jump out of nowhere. "Enfant!" Meg gasped.

At once Toy and Petite joined the dog whose name meant Child. Toy wore the gun belt and hat he had worn to the tea. Child wore a red bow; Petite, her mesh coat.

Mrs. Glynn said, "Hello, Meg, Kerry." She was again the cool person they had met at the pet shop. She held out a small box and said, "I have a gift for you, Meg."

Puzzled, Meg took the box. Her fingers pulled at the ribbon. "Thank—you," she said.

Above her, at the lighted kitchen window, Mrs. Wilson held up a cautioning finger, her face grim.

Meg looked around. She saw Thunder. He was sitting on top of the rose trellis, twitching his black tail. At the foot of the trellis, the three poodles danced on hind legs. The big cat hissed.

"Thunder," Meg scolded lovingly. "Those little dogs won't hurt you. Come down." But Thunder did not obey.

"Open your gift," Mrs. Glynn urged.

"Oh—yes." With her attention divided between the poodles and her cat, Meg tore open the package. Curled in a nest of wrapping paper was the soft leather band. It was covered with small metal bells.

"The collar I wanted," Meg said in real surprise. "Why? I thought—I mean—" Meg knew she was receiving a gift badly. She smiled and said, "Thank you, Mrs. Glynn. I like it very much, and so will Thunder."

"Let's put it on him and see how it fits," Mrs. Glynn said. She walked to the trellis and reached for the big cat. He swatted her hand and left a long, red streak. "You beast!" she said angrily.

At once she turned a smile on Meg. She said, "I'm not used to cats. My little ones don't scratch, you know. You'll have to put the collar on Thunder."

Meg coaxed. She made the soft, loving sounds that usually drew Thunder from secret hiding places. He would not come down.

Mrs. Glynn picked up the three leashes. She said, "You *will* put the collar on him?"

"Yes-s, of course," Meg said, softening and slurring her words in the Virginia way. She stood close to Kerry while the actress crossed the lawn. "I wonder why she gave me a present," Meg said. "She doesn't like cats."

Kerry shrugged. "What do you care? You have the collar you wanted."

"It is pretty, isn't it?" Meg's dimples popped into her cheeks when she smiled. She gave the collar a little jiggle. There was no tinkle, just a soft rattling sound. Meg shook it again. She said, "I'm sure it jingled like little bells."

Kerry wrinkled her nose. "That's more of a thud sound. Probably it didn't suit that persnickety Mrs. Glynn. She brought it to you to get rid of it."

"Oh, well," Meg said airily. "It's pretty. Thunder

isn't going to like wearing it, no matter what kind of a sound it makes. But he can't sneak up on the cardinals when he wears this collar."

Meg coaxed Thunder from the rose trellis. Before she buckled it around his neck, she shook the collar again. "Nope," she said sadly. "No tinkle."

Soon it was completely dark outside. Meg, Kerry, and the Wilsons sat on the patio. They watched fireflies that glowed like bits of fallen stars. Meg noticed that Kerry giggled several times. That meant she had forgotten about Cissie's trouble for a little while.

As relaxed as a kitten, Meg curled in her favorite lawn chair. She thought of happy things: Dad's chuckle, Uncle Hal, books, watercolors, ballet—

Uh-oh! Ballet. She must find those slippers to-morrow. She could not skip dance practice two days in a row.

Mrs. Wilson said, "I called your mother, Kerry. She says you may stay all night with Meg."

"Thank you, Mrs. Wilson," Kerry said. "Ma'am would have missed me at nose-counting time. That's when Sir gets out his little black book and calls roll.''

"Silly!'' Meg giggled at Kerry's nonsense. It was at moments like this that she ached, a little, for the family she did not have.

Finally even Mrs. Wilson patted a yawn and forgot about the diamonds. Meg and Kerry went upstairs to Meg's room. Thunder followed. He stopped on the stair landing to scratch the collar around his neck.

"Never mind, Thunder,'' Meg said. "You'll get used to it. You have no idea how many scoldings that collar will save you.''

In Meg's pink and white room, Thunder curled in his flat basket on the window seat.

Twin beds fitted into a corner like the halves of a sectional sofa. Meg turned down the covers for Kerry and patted the pillow. She liked having her head near Kerry's while she slept.

After the girls were in bed, Thunder made muttering noises. Kerry said, "He hates that collar.''

"Mmm,'' Meg said sleepily.

6
NIGHT FRIGHT

Suddenly Meg sat up in bed. For an instant she did not know where she was or what had wakened her.

"Mer-awrrh!" screamed Thunder. His Siamese war cry was enough to wake all the neighbors on Culpepper Road.

"Thunder!" she cried. She turned on her lamp. She saw that Kerry, too, was wide awake. Thunder lunged at the window and screamed again.

Through chattering teeth, Kerry said, "Th-There's something out th-there."

"Or . . . somebody," Meg said slowly. "That was Thunder's own special I-don't-like-people cry."

Afraid, but determined to protect her beloved pet, Meg tiptoed across the floor.

Thunder slapped the screen so hard his claws stuck in the wire. Meg lifted his heavy body to loosen the claws. "What is it, Thunder?" she asked anxiously.

Kerry crossed the room to see if Meg needed help. They moved close together when they heard the muffled sound of a car's motor.

"There *was* someone out there," Meg said. She dug her fingers into Thunder's fur.

Kerry hugged herself with fright. "Mrs. Partlow's house last night, and your house tonight. Meg, what do they want?"

"I wish I knew," Meg said. She leaned against the window screen and peered down on the dark side lawn.

Whenever Meg thought hard, she patted her leg with three quick taps. Pat. Pat. Pat. She tapped several times before she checked the locks on the windows. She found nothing wrong.

Meg even locked the hall door before she turned

out the light. She made room for Thunder on her bed, but he didn't settle down. He paced the floor all night. Once he screamed. Neither Meg nor Kerry slept well.

At breakfast the next morning, Mr. Wilson asked, "Meg, what in tarnation got into that tiger last night?"

In the morning light, last night's fright was unreal. Had someone really tried to break in? Had a car been parked in the deep shadows?

Meg was not sure of the answers, but she meant to find out. She said, "Excuse us. We have something to do."

Under the table, Meg kicked Kerry's ankle. Kerry said, "Excuse us. Something to do."

Thunder followed the girls down the hall, which ran through the middle of the house. He grumbled and bumped the floor with his tail.

"I'll feed you later, Thunder," Meg said. "Right now we're in a hurry."

"What are we hurrying to do?" Kerry asked.

"You'll see." Meg cut across the lawn near the

bowed window at the front of the house. In the middle of the yard, she turned to face the window of her room. She walked backward. At the edge of the road, she said, "Here."

Impatiently Kerry asked, "Here, what?"

"Here's where we look for car tracks."

The girls studied the dirt road. All tracks looked alike, but Meg noticed crushed grass. A heavy wheel had rolled on the lawn.

"So," Meg said, "there *was* a car."

Meg and Kerry zigzagged across the lawn. They found no footprints in the grass. But at the edge

of the flower bed, between the living-room window and the patio, someone had stood long enough to smoke three cigarettes.

"Mr. Wilson smokes a pipe," Meg said.

"His feet are smaller, too," Kerry said.

"A man must have watched us while we were on the patio," Meg said worriedly. "If he wanted to break into the house, why didn't he do it while we were outside?"

"Maybe what he wanted was outside, too," Kerry said. She hugged herself when she said, "I don't like to be spied on. It gives me shivers."

Across the creek, the Carmody bell rang. "Walk part way with me?" Kerry asked. "I must go take care of Chappie."

"And keep your eyes on Cissie," Meg said.

The girls cut across Mrs. Partlow's place. Several people were in the garden. A number of official-looking cars were lined up in the driveway. One of them was a television truck. Meg knew this meant the diamonds had probably not been found.

It meant, too, that Cissie had not been suspected. Many men would not come from the city to hunt for one little girl's playhouse.

Meg set up her practice bar on the patio in the shade. She put on her ragged, old pink slippers and began limbering-up exercises.

Usually Thunder walked the bar or jumped at her toes while she worked. This morning he did not show up, even when Meg called.

She could hear the buzz of Mrs. Wilson's vacuum cleaner. In the garage, Mr. Wilson whistled. Birds stole food from Thunder's red dish. That made

Meg feel lonesome. They did not dare steal food when Thunder was around. Where could he be?

A little jerkily, Meg reached for the high bar. Then she almost fell. A white fluff darted around the corner of the house. Brown and black followed.

"Don't stop," a cool voice said. "I just dropped by to see if Thunder likes his collar." Mrs. Glynn kept a firm hand on the leashes of her dressed-up poodles. She looked around and sounded annoyed when she said, "I don't see your cat."

"He's off rambling," Meg said. She went on with her exercise, but kept her eyes on the dogs. She asked, "Are you going to a party?"

Mrs. Glynn laughed. "You noticed Petite's new coat? She likes to look pretty. Oh! Don't worry about her crown. I'm sure it's safe. I can pick it up if she bumps it off."

"Yes, ma'am," Meg said politely. The dogs sat in a row. When they could behave so nicely, Meg felt it was too bad they had ruined the tea. To be polite she said, "I like Child's new bow."

Mrs. Glynn looked into the flower beds. She

looked into the great oaks and catalpas. She asked, "Should you let Thunder go off alone? After all, he is a very valuable cat."

"Cats always go out alone," Meg said. "He can take care of himself."

"Oh, I'm sure he can," Mrs. Glynn said quickly. "I was thinking of the collar. Should he wear it out of doors?"

"Why not?" Meg asked. "That's where the birds are. I wanted the collar to warn the cardinals. He likes to chase them."

"He might hang himself on a limb when he jumps," Mrs. Glynn said. "In the night, I worried about that. So I came to warn you."

"Thank you," Meg said uneasily.

When Mrs. Glynn left with her dogs, Meg telephoned Kerry. Kerry answered from the barn. Meg asked, "Is Thunder hunting mice in your barn?"

"I haven't seen him," Kerry answered.

"Meg, dear," Mrs. Wilson called. "Will you take a plate of hot cookies to Miss Upshur, please? Oh, my, oh, my, that poor woman is fit to be tied. She

was the first one the police talked to. They seem to think she made too much of a to-do. She asked to see the diamonds and try them on and all.''

Meg took the cookies from Mrs. Wilson. She asked, "Have the police been here yet?"

"Oh, my, no. I'd be all aflutter. Miss Upshur called me when they left her house."

Meg smiled as she left the house. She did not have to ask Mrs. Wilson what had happened next. She knew. Mrs. Wilson had called Miss Culpepper, who had called Mrs. Wayburn, who had called Mrs.

Hosey. That's the way news got around in Hidden Springs. Neighbors were longtime friends. No matter what the news, everyone knew it.

Meg pulled her dark brows into a frown. "So," she wondered, "how can a mystery grow here? A mystery is a secret. Nothing is secret in Hidden Springs. Nothing but Cissie's playhouse, that is."

Miss Upshur lived on Upland Way. The road lay between Old Bridge Road and the highway to Washington, D.C. It was a dirt road. Flowers grew between its ruts. With each step, Meg watched for Thunder. She did not see him.

Meg found her elderly friend in her garden. Miss Upshur was hoeing carrots. She talked to herself in twittery, birdlike cries and chirps. When she saw Meg, she burst out, "That detective asked *me* if *I* took Hannah's diamonds. Can you imagine how I felt? In all my born days, I've never stolen a pin!"

"I'm sure you haven't, Miss Upshur," Meg said earnestly. She gave the tiny woman Mrs. Wilson's cookies.

While they ate cookies, Miss Upshur twittered

on. "I just wanted to see how it feels to wear something so lovely. *That's* why I asked to try on the diamonds."

Miss Upshur cried. Then she ate a cookie. Then she hoed her carrots. When Meg started back down Upland Way, the tiny woman was still hoeing and talking and crying.

Meg felt sorry for her. She wished she could help, but all she could think of was Thunder. Where was he? Was he safe?

Meg met Mrs. Glynn and the poodles on their way back to the house they rented from Miss Upshur. "Have you found your cat?" Mrs. Glynn asked.

"No, ma'am," Meg answered. While she tried to figure out why Mrs. Glynn kept on asking the same question each time they met, Meg patted her leg. Pat. Pat. Pat.

Suddenly the dogs began to race around and around. Mrs. Glynn grabbed their red leashes and ordered them to sit. She looked so cross that Meg worried all the way home.

7
A CRIMINAL
AMONG US?

Before Meg reached the front door, Mrs. Wilson called, "Hurry, Meg! Your father is on the phone."

Meg ran. She shouted gladly into the telephone, "I've missed you, Dad. Are you coming home?"

"Not for a few days, honey. I called to ask what's going on out there in Hidden Springs. Mrs. Partlow's story is on TV and radio and in the papers."

Dad paused. Then in slow, measured tones he said, "Margaret Ashley Duncan, are you mixed up in this case?"

"I'm trying to help," Meg said.

"Margaret," Dad said firmly. "You leave criminal-chasing to the police. I want to find you in one piece when I get home.''

"Criminals?" Meg gasped. "Dad, I'm not hunting for criminals! I'm hunting for Cissie and Thunder and my ballet slippers!''

"Good," Dad said. "Love you, honey."

"I love you, too," Meg answered. Tears hung on her dark lashes as she left the house. Hearing Dad's voice made her feel lonesome, right to the tip of her toes. And Thunder was not here to purr away the hurt. "Th-Thunder?" she called shakily. No sound. Not a throat grumble. Not a tail thump. Nothing.

All day the police went in and out of the neighbors' houses. They asked questions.

Mr. Hosey came to the Duncan house. He said, "I hate to suspect a neighbor. On the other hand, Mrs. Glynn is the only stranger. She found an earring, however, and she asked to be searched. Does that sound guilty?

"How could she take the diamonds in plain sight of everyone? We looked at the dress she wore that afternoon. No pockets.'' He sighed loudly. ''Who else is there?''

Meg wanted to tell him about the man who smoked cigarettes, but Kerry came to help look for Thunder. Diamonds mattered far less to Meg than Thunder.

Cissie played in the Carmody backyard all afternoon. Kerry and Meg crawled under bushes and hedges, even under the front porch and into the barn loft. They found nothing. Not Thunder. Not Meg's slippers. Not even an earring.

Ma'am asked Meg to stay for supper. Later in Kerry's room, the girls turned on the radio.

''Odd things are happening in Hidden Springs,'' the announcer said. ''Mrs. Glynn reports that her poodle's crown is missing.''

''Meg, you warned her,'' Kerry said.

The announcer went on, ''She says the crown is set with a small diamond. Also, Mr. Wayburn, owner of the local pet shop, reports a missing birdcage. No birds. Just a cage. It was taken from his station wagon while parked near the Partlow gate on Culpepper Road.''

"What *is* going on?" Meg asked worriedly.

"Ssh," Kerry warned. "I thought I heard—"

"Thunder?" Meg cried. "Let's go!"

Carrying flashlights, Meg, Kerry, and Mike walked back and forth between the house and Cricket Run. Several times they heard a mournful cry. It sounded both near and far away.

Meg was so upset that Kerry led the way across the bridge to search a wider area.

Meg whispered, "There's another light."

"Two," Mike said. "Over at Partlow's."

"One light follows the other," Meg said.

"Let's follow both," Mike said.

At once the three friends hurried down the road. Like fireflies, the five lights bobbed in the dark. Meg managed to turn her light on the leader. It was Mrs. Glynn. The second light disappeared at once.

"Maybe she's hunting for Petite's crown," Kerry said.

"Why did Mrs. Glynn run when you turned on the light?" Mike asked.

"I—don't know," Meg said slowly. "I wonder. . . ."

Just after sunrise on Thursday morning, Meg and Kerry went to Mrs. Partlow's garden. Inside the house they heard Callie.

"We're snooping," Kerry said uneasily. "We haven't found a thing out of place. We don't know why Mrs. Glynn was here."

"I want to look at that window," Meg said. "The break-in Monday night was the first trouble."

Meg looked at the sill, the wall, and the stone foundation. When she rose, she held out a scrap of pink velvet. "Let's go talk to Callie," she said.

Callie liked children. She gave Meg and Kerry cinnamon buns. While they ate, Meg asked, "Does Mrs. Partlow wear pink velvet?"

"Yes. But, glory be, she hasn't worn it since Christmas," Callie said.

As they started back toward Meg's house, Kerry said, "Child had a pink bow."

"I thought of that," Meg said. "But I found this scrap on the wrong side of the house. The tea was near the holly bushes on the other side."

Slowly Meg went home alone.

She opened the patio door just in time to see the front door close. The Wilsons seldom used the front door. Meg ran past the kitchen, dining room, and library doors. By the time she had opened the heavy front door, no one was in sight.

While she stood there, a car pulled away from the edge of the road down near Mrs. Partlow's gate. It was headed toward Hidden Springs, going fast. The driver was a man.

"I know he was in our house," Meg muttered. "What do *we* have that he wants? Something he didn't find at Mrs. Partlow's? What could that *be?*"

More than a little frightened, Meg called out. Mrs. Wilson came down the stairs. Mr. Wilson came through the back door.

When Meg told them about the man, Mr. Wilson called the police. On the noon radio news the announcer asked, "What comes next? Have we a criminal among us?"

Criminal, Meg thought while she ate a tuna fish sandwich. Dad had used that word, too. Thinking about it, shadows seemed to grow where no shadows had been.

Meg put on her ragged slippers. She went out to her exercise bar on the patio. When she worked, she could think. And Meg needed to think.

Was a criminal loose in Hidden Springs? If so, it must be the man in the car. Cissie might take the diamonds, but she would not break into houses. What did both Mrs. Partlow and the Duncans have that a criminal might want? Meg could not even guess.

Mr. Wilson was at work in the shrubs. He said, "The missus went up to Miss Upshur's. She needs cheering up. Thought I'd tell you. We're keeping our eyes open for that tiger."

"Thank you, Mr. Wilson," Meg said.

Meg wished somebody would cheer up Margaret Ashley Duncan. She started her record player. Behind her a cool voice said, "Have you found Thunder yet?"

There was Mrs. Glynn with her three dogs. She asked the same question in the same worried voice.

Meg wondered why the woman bothered to ask.
She did not like Thunder. She had called him a
beast.

Around the corner of the house came Cissie,
dragging Cecil, her rag doll. She was followed by
the Carmody dog.

Cissie ran to Toy. She sat on her heels to look
at Toy's gun belt. Almost at once, she unbuckled
the belt with the holster.

"You little snooper!" Mrs. Glynn shouted. "Give
me that!" She grabbed, but Cissie ran with the
holster in her hands.

At once there was a tangle of red leashes, poodles,

Cissie's doll, and Mrs. Glynn's long legs and high heels.

Mr. Wilson ran across the yard. He tried to untangle the dogs.

Mrs. Glynn shrieked, "Mind your own business!"

"Okay, if that's the way you want it," Mr. Wilson said gruffly.

"First, Petite's crown! Now, Jouet's gun belt!" Mrs. Glynn shouted angrily. "Is nothing safe from thieves out here in the sticks?"

"Cissie isn't a thief!" Meg shouted back. "She just wanted to look at Toy's gun."

"Where," Mrs. Glynn shrieked, "where *is* that child?"

Cissie had disappeared. Dragging her dogs by their leashes, Mrs. Glynn stamped off to catch her.

Meg ran to the telephone to call Kerry. She got her on the extension phone in the barn. "Find Cissie," Meg begged. "Mrs. Glynn is chasing her."

"She can't chase a Carmody!" Kerry yelled.

8
VERY IMPORTANT NEWS

Kerry and Mike raced through the meadow and over the bridge behind the barn. Meg met them in the field behind her own house.

"Where'd that woman go?" Mike yelled.

Meg grinned. "The wrong way," she said. "I saw Cissie go through Mrs. Partlow's hedge. Mrs. Glynn is tramping around in the bushes along Cricket Run."

"Good," Kerry said tartly. "I hope she breaks a heel."

"But—" Meg said, "Cissie did take Toy's holster. Mrs. Glynn wants it back."

Kerry groaned. "Oh, no! Slippers. Diamonds.

Thunder. And now, Toy's holster's gone. Everything disappears.''

Mike said hopefully, ''There are lots of places we haven't looked.''

''Name one,'' Kerry grumbled.

Dragging their heels, the three friends went back to Meg's patio to plan where to search next. They found Cissie in Mr. Wilson's chair. She held out Meg's pink ballet slippers and smiled sweetly.

''Th-Thank you, Cissie!'' Meg said. Almost speechless with surprise, she looked down at the slippers. One looked fatter than the other. She put in her hand and pulled out—

''Mrs. Partlow's snood!'' Kerry gasped. She began to cry. Meg felt so sorry for Kerry that she cried, too. Even Mike sniffed loudly.

''I knew she t-took them, but I h-h-hoped she didn't,'' Kerry sobbed.

Meg gulped, ''We should be glad, not sad! We have the snood. Cissie will show us where to find the rest of the diamonds, won't you, Cissie, please?''

''I don't see any diamonds,'' Mike said.

"Just look," Meg said. She spread the hairnet, then gasped, "They're gone! Someone cut them out. See the holes in the net?"

"Cissie, where are they?" Kerry cried.

Cissie pointed at Meg's slippers. She said sweetly, "I bringed them back to Meg."

"Diamonds, not slippers!" Kerry said. "Shiny stones. For rings. Where are they?"

Cissie would say nothing. In a few minutes, Kerry and Mike followed Cissie home. They argued about whether or not they should tell Ma'am about Cissie and the diamonds.

"I knew nice people would be hurt," said Meg unhappily.

At that moment, Mr. Wilson asked for help. Meg went around the house to hold the ladder for him. While he mended a shutter, she stood by the fireplace. She saw that the vines had been pulled apart near the bricks.

For a happy second she thought she had found Thunder's hiding place. She reached in and touched something that felt like wire. When she pulled it out, she found that she held Petite's crown!

"Oh, that Cissie!" This must be one of her hiding places. Was nothing safe from her? Ballet slippers, diamonds, and now Petite's crown.

Out of curiosity, Meg reached in again. This time she pulled out Toy's gun and Child's pink velvet bow.

"How would Cissie have gotten these?" Meg wondered. She thought hard and tapped her leg. Pat. Pat. Pat.

She stared at vines and ground. She saw that the flower bed had been punched with holes like those under Mrs. Partlow's window. There was no sign of Cissie, not even a footprint.

As Meg turned away, she saw a piece of leather at the edge of one of the holes. She picked it up, started to drop it, then looked more closely. It was the tap from a high heel.

Mrs. Wilson wore sensible heels. The women of the neighborhood walked and gardened. They seldom wore high heels out of doors. But Mrs. Glynn *always* wore high heels.

All of these things belonged to those dogs. So, Meg reasoned, Mrs. Glynn could have put the things in the vines. But if she had hidden them, why had she reported the crown missing?

And *why* did she chase Cissie for an empty holster? Here was the gun.

Meg's jacket had large pockets. She put the snood and crown in one pocket, the gun and pink bow in the other. Then she called Kerry on the telephone. "I have VERY IMPORTANT NEWS. Meet me at the meadow bridge," she said.

As Meg walked across the field, she looked at each clump of field daisies. She hoped to find Thunder sneaking up on a mouse. It was Thursday, and almost suppertime. Wednesday morning seemed long ago. Did Thunder have food? Water? Was he even—alive?

Tears filled Meg's dark eyes. She pushed that fear down deep. She watched Kerry cross the meadow, blond hair glowing in the sunlight.

Willows grew along the creek. Near the end of the log bridge, something white moved. Meg squinted, then gulped in surprise. That was Petite in her shining coat, glittering like a Christmas tree! Toy and Child sat beside her. Mrs. Glynn was not in sight.

Watching for both Mrs. Glynn and Cissie, Meg walked up to the three poodles. They watched her with eyes like round, black berries. While she tried to think why the dogs might be in this spot, Meg patted her leg. Pat. Pat. Pat.

Suddenly Mrs. Glynn's poodles began a silent race. Around and around they ran together, as if on cue. Meg could see they ran in a pattern like a figure eight.

Kerry ran to catch the dogs. She hugged them.

The dogs wiggled away. She said, "They aren't very friendly, are they?"

"Kerry," Meg said, "I think these dogs perform with some signal. They seem to expect me to tell them what to do next."

"Nobody told them to run," Kerry argued.

"But I might have done something they thought was a signal. Up on the road to Miss Upshur's, the dogs ran. It made Mrs. Glynn cross."

While she tried to remember exactly what she had done, Meg beat time with her fingers. Pat. Pat. Pat.

At once the dogs raced in circles.

"That's it!" Meg cried. "Their other signals are voice signals. This one is a hand signal. Three pats means *run.*"

"I don't get it," Kerry said bluntly.

"Just catch Toy," Meg said. She caught Child while Kerry caught Toy's leash. Petite, whose name meant Little One, kept right on running. Her coat flashed light.

When Meg picked up Petite, her fingers felt lumps

107

under the coat. She fumbled for the zipper of Petite's fancy costume.

"Mrs. Glynn would have a fit if she saw you monkeying with her dogs," Kerry warned.

"There's—something—under—here," Meg said. *Zip-p-p!* Light glinted and sparkled when she opened the shining mesh coat.

"Mrs. Partlow's NECKLACE!" Meg gasped. "It's here!"

"Why is Petite wearing it under her coat?" Kerry asked in a scared whisper.

Shakily Meg zipped up Petite's shining coat. With a quick look around, she put the necklace in the pocket with the snood. She told Kerry, "Let's run!"

The loft of the Carmody barn was a favorite talking and thinking place. Meg and Kerry sat side by side on a bale of hay. In a low voice, Meg told about the hiding place in the vines.

Then she put the crown, pink bow, gun, snood, and necklace on the hay. Even in the dim light the necklace glowed with diamond-fire. "Isn't it beautiful?" Meg whispered.

"Hide it, quick," Kerry begged. So Meg put the things back into her pockets.

Kerry said, "If Mrs. Glynn tramped in your yard, she could have broken into Mrs. Partlow's house Monday night. We found holes under her window, too."

"Yes-s," Meg said. "If Child guarded, and something surprised her, she could have torn her pink velvet bow. Mrs. Glynn might have hidden the bow so she wouldn't be connected with the break-in."

"What did Mrs. Glynn want?" Kerry asked.

Meg answered Kerry's question with a question. "What did she get? Mrs. Partlow's diamonds."

Kerry twisted her fingers in knots. She said, "I *hope* Cissie didn't take them, but we must be wrong about Mrs. Glynn. She had no pockets. Cissie is little. She crawled through the flowers. We found her footprints. She had the snood, too. Don't forget that."

"I know," Meg said worriedly. "There has to be an answer. I'm sure Mrs. Glynn gave a *hand* signal to make those dogs run. When they quieted down,

110

the diamonds were gone. We found the necklace under Petite's coat. No one but Mrs. Glynn touches those dogs. So she must have put the necklace on Petite.''

''Just think,'' Kerry said, shaking her blond head. ''With police all over the place, Petite's been walking around with that necklace.''

''Who'd expect a poodle to wear diamonds?'' Meg said.

''Mrs. Glynn told us Petite wears diamonds,'' Kerry said, ''that day when we met her in the pet shop.''

''And she told everybody when she reported the crown stolen,'' Meg said. ''That was pretty smart! The police thought she had been robbed. Who would suspect her of doing the robbing?''

''But how did she do it? We were at the party. We know Mrs. Glynn and her poodles bounced around in the middle of things.''

''I don't know,'' Meg said. She stood up and said, ''I'm going to take this necklace to Constable Hosey. Then I'm going to find Thunder if it takes all night.

112

For some reason, Mrs. Glynn is interested in him. If she's a criminal—"

"Criminal?" Kerry cried. Her blue eyes widened with fright. "Meg! That woman has been hunting for Cissie for hours. What can we *do?* If Mrs. Glynn goes back to her dogs and finds that necklace is gone, Cissie might get hurt!"

"There's a phone downstairs," Meg said. "We'll call Constable Hosey."

"What good will that do? Cissie isn't here," Kerry said in despair.

"She will be," Meg said. "We'll ring the bell."

As the girls hurried toward the large bell, Meg said, "One thing bothers me. If Mrs. Glynn had the diamonds, and she knew where Petite's crown was, why was she in Mrs. Partlow's garden last night? And why were there two flashlights?"

"I'm so s-s-scared, I can't think!" Kerry said. "Let's ring that bell!"

9

TELL SIR
WE NEED HIM

While Kerry rang the bell, Meg called the constable on the barn telephone. She told him, "I have the necklace and crown. I'm scared. Will you meet me at Old Stone Bridge?"

"Meg, Cissie is crying!" Kerry shouted.

Hastily Meg said, "I have to go now."

In the barnyard, Meg and Kerry listened. Cissie's voice sounded both near and far away. "It kind of echoes," Meg said.

"Like in a barrel," Kerry said.

Quickly both girls scanned the neat white fences, watering troughs, and green meadow; the backyard, vegetable garden, and playground behind the farmhouse; and the bushes and willows that grew along Cricket Run. They could see nothing that would act as a sounding board for an echo.

"I think she's near the road," Kerry said. "She's really crying. Let's run!"

Answering the bell, Mike climbed over a fence.

Meg shouted, "Cissie is in trouble!"

Mike, Kerry, and Meg raced through garden and yard, then around the Carmody house. A long lawn sloped toward the road. Several very old oaks and a tangle of bushes and willows almost hid the stone bridge. Something else was almost hidden, too. A car. Meg saw it and pointed.

The bridge crossed Cricket Run halfway between the Carmody and Partlow houses.

Near the road, Cissie crawled out of the bushes. When she stood, she tried to run. She shouted, "You go 'way! My bell's ringing."

Right behind Cissie, Mrs. Glynn pushed through the bushes. Her black hair caught on branches and sagged in witch's loops. She jerked free of the bush and dashed forward. She yelled, "You sticky-fingered

little monster. Give me that holster!''

Stooping as they ran near the bushes, Meg, Kerry, and Mike hurried to help Cissie. Meg was close enough to see Mrs. Glynn grab the rag doll, Cecil. She pulled the gun belt from the doll's body, then threw the doll. Quickly she tore open the holster.

In a voice far from calm, Mrs. Glynn yelled, *''Where is that snood?''*

Crying, Cissie ran back to pick up her beloved Cecil. Mrs. Glynn grabbed Cissie's long, blond hair.

Mike shot forward, fists clenched. ''You can't pull Cissie's hair!'' he yelled. ''She's a Carmody!''

Startled, Mrs. Glynn swung around. As she turned, she slapped Mike—so hard that he fell. Cissie shrieked in terror. She hugged her doll. Instead of running home, she ran back toward the bridge.

Kerry yelled, ''Cissie! You're going the wrong way!'' She swerved to help Mike.

Meg grabbed Kerry's arm. ''Mike can take care of himself,'' she said. ''Let's follow Cissie.''

''O-Okay,'' Kerry gasped. ''What's the matter with that woman? Is she crazy?''

"L-Like a fox," Meg panted as she ran. "She thought she'd find the snood where she put it in the holster. But it isn't there. Cissie put it in my slipper."

Kerry grabbed Meg's arm and spun her around. "Why would she want that old snood with holes in it and no diamonds?" she asked.

"I don't know," Meg said. "But she wants it, that's for sure."

"Ssh, I hear something," Kerry warned.

"Cissie?" Meg began. Then her lips stretched in a wide smile. A warm glow crept from the tips of her toes and spread to her heart. "Thunder!" she cried happily. "I hear him, Kerry. He's alive!"

"Yeah, but mad," Kerry said as Thunder's Siamese war cry rolled out, doubled by an echo. "He must be in a barrel."

"*I* know!" Meg said, tingling with excitement. "He's under the bridge!" Meg pushed through the bushes to get to Thunder. She saw that Mike was hanging onto Mrs. Glynn. The woman slapped and kicked in her effort to follow Cissie.

Cissie came from under the bridge. The small

girl bent under the weight she carried. Cecil was in one hand. In the other she carried a birdcage.

In the birdcage sat Thunder, so cramped for space his head touched the top of the cage. His sharp teeth bit his wire prison.

"Cissie took Thunder and hid him under the bridge!" Meg shouted.

"In Mr. Wayburn's birdcage!" Kerry added.

A man slid down the slope at the end of the bridge. He reached Cissie ahead of Kerry and Meg, who were slowed down by prickly bushes that clutched at their hair and clothes.

Mrs. Glynn limped down the slope, fighting off Mike.

The man took the birdcage from Cissie. Just as he unlatched the door of the cage, Meg shrieked, "That's my cat! Don't touch him!" She beat the man's arms and chest with her fists.

"Give me that collar!" Mrs. Glynn yelled.

"Over my dead body!" the man shouted back. He tried to pull the leather collar over Thunder's black ears.

"Be careful! You'll choke him," Meg cried.

The man growled, "Who cares? He's just a cat." He held Thunder tightly while he tried to unbuckle the leather collar.

Thunder had been caged long enough to make his bad temper even worse. He kicked. A front paw came free. He ripped the man's bare hand. He bit the tip of a finger.

With a shout, the man threw the cat. Thunder leaped. Away he went, black tail in the air. He shot up the first tree in sight. Meg shouted, "Go, Thunder, go!"

Both Mrs. Glynn and the strange man turned on Meg. "Get that collar!" Mrs. Glynn ordered angrily.

"If you give it to her, I'll break your neck!" the man yelled. He shook Meg fiercely.

Both Mike and Kerry tried to help Meg. Mike clung to the man's legs. Kerry held Mrs. Glynn's hands. Cissie left the empty birdcage and ran to answer the Carmody bell.

"You better come," she called back to Kerry and Mike. "Ma'am says so."

"Tell Sir we need him!" Mike shouted.

One of the man's hands shot out. He hit Mrs. Glynn instead of Mike. She yelled, "How *dare* you strike me, Bill Purdy!"

Down the slope at the end of the bridge came Constable Hosey. He motioned with his gun. "What's going on here?" he demanded.

Instantly the man smiled. He fixed his tie. Mrs. Glynn tried to smooth her hair. As she did so, a small black box fell from her bun. Mike bent to pick it up, but she pushed him so hard he bumped his nose on Constable Hosey's knee.

"Give me that!" Mrs. Glynn snapped.

"Give it to me, Mike," the constable said. "Is this the kind of treatment you young'uns have been getting from these people?"

"Worse, Mr. Hosey," Kerry said hotly. "Mrs. Glynn pulled Cissie's hair, and what's-his-name—"

"Bill Purdy," Meg put in.

"—shook Meg and threw Thunder," Kerry finished, her eyes blazing.

"Looks like I'll have to take you two down to the

station to cool off," Constable Hosey said.

"Look, Officer," Bill said. "There's been a misunderstanding. I was just—"

"—hunting for Meg's cat!" Mrs. Glynn said, smiling brightly. "I knew how upset she had been, so I was trying to be friendly."

Meg had been listening and watching. She pulled the crown, necklace, and snood from her pockets. She said, "While she was being so *friendly* to me, her white poodle was wearing Mrs. Partlow's diamonds."

Mrs. Glynn's hand flashed out, but Meg ducked the blow. "You—little—thief!" Mrs. Glynn said through gritted teeth.

Sternly the constable asked, "Meg, where did you get that necklace?"

Suddenly the man, Bill Purdy, tackled Constable Hosey, football fashion. Both men went down in a tangle of arms, legs, handcuffs, and gun.

The front door of the Carmody house opened. Sir leaped down the steps two at a time. On down the sloping lawn he came with a roar.

10
IN PLAIN SIGHT

While the constable and Bill fought, Mike kicked the gun away from Bill's reach.

The black box rolled, and Mrs. Glynn picked it up. She ran toward the car.

"Catch her, Sir!" Meg shouted.

Kerry's husky father caught the actress before she reached the road. He brought her back just as the constable won the fight.

Constable Hosey locked the handcuffs on the man's wrists. He said sternly, "That's for attacking an officer. When I find out why you're bothering our young 'uns, I may just throw away the key."

Bill Purdy glared.

Sir sidestepped Mrs. Glynn's kicking feet. "Please tell me what's going on here," Sir drawled in complete amazement.

"We've caught the diamond thief, Sir," Meg explained. "We thought it was Cissie, but we made a mistake."

"Cissie?" Sir roared.

Quickly Kerry said, "We didn't think she stole them, Sir. We thought she took them to play with. She really did take the snood."

"And Meg's slippers," Mike said.

"And Thunder in Mr. Wayburn's birdcage, and Toy's holster," Meg said. Her voice sank to a whisper. A kind person was being hurt. Worry lines grew around Sir's mouth.

"True, Cissie has been a busy girl," the constable said. "But I think I'll look at the black box. Mrs. Glynn is anxious to keep it."

"It's personal," Mrs. Glynn said icily. "I wear it to hold my bun in place."

Loudly Kerry whispered, "Isn't any part of her real? She pastes on her eyelashes and stuffs her bun."

The officer rolled the box in his hand. He squeezed. A lid sank. He lifted out a small object. The lid raised again. Meg, Kerry, and Mike crowded close to watch.

"Mrs. Partlow's EARRING!" Meg said.

Sir and the constable whistled. Bill Purdy snarled at Mrs. Glynn.

"Mrs. Partlow will be glad to see this," the constable said. "But how it got in Mrs. Glynn's bun, I don't know."

"I do," Meg said eagerly. "Her hair was wrapped around this box. It's a kind of trap. I saw her touch

her hair, but I didn't see her push the earring in. I looked at the other earring. She held it in front of her."

"The oldest trick in the book," the constable said. "If you want to hide a thing, put it out in plain sight."

"That's why Petite's coat was so fancy," Meg said. "Mrs. Glynn looped the necklace around Petite's neck. It didn't show up on all those shiny beads and sequins. Later she put it under Petite's coat."

"By then people were tired of looking at the dogs," Kerry said tartly.

"She put the snood in Toy's holster, then came back to look for the gun she dropped," Meg said.

"Or maybe to get the other earring," Kerry said accusingly.

Bill Purdy laughed harshly. "Some plan! Even a kid figures it out."

"Shut up!" Mrs. Glynn flared back. "It would have worked if you hadn't showed up. What was the big idea, following me?"

"I can smell a double cross. You planned to get

128

away with the ice by ditching it and picking it up when the heat was off."

"Ice?" Kerry asked Meg.

"Diamonds," Meg said. She whirled on the man. Remembering the fright he had caused her, she asked hotly, "Why were you in my house?"

"Ask my lawyer," Bill said coldly.

The actress smiled, as if she knew something she was not telling. Or, Meg thought, as if she had not lost everything.

Meg gave the necklace, snood, crown, Toy's gun, Child's pink bow, and even the heel tap to Constable Hosey.

She said, "I'm sorry about the damaged snood. No one wears them now. Maybe Mrs. Partlow won't need it for the wedding tomorrow night."

"Mrs. Partlow's reward will go to you young'uns," the constable said. Carefully he put the jewels in his pockets.

"We'll get something for Cissie," Meg said. "To let her know we're sorry we thought she took the diamonds."

"A bell for her neck, maybe?" Kerry asked. She grinned widely, but tears hung on her blond lashes. Mike blew his nose. The worry lines left Sir's red face. Meg felt warm, right to the tips of her toes. The Carmody name was clear again.

The constable reached for the birdcage. He said, "I'll take this back to Wayburn."

"Cissie must have liked that cage, or she wouldn't have taken it," Meg said. "Let's buy it and give it to her."

"With white mice in it," Mike said.

Kerry frowned at Mike. She said, "That noisy canary, Meg! Mr. Wayburn wants to get rid of it. With that bird in Cissie's playhouse, she can't hide from us."

"Okay, Mike?" Meg asked.

"Okay," Mike said good-naturedly.

"Good," the constable said. "I'll leave the cage. I'll tell Wayburn you young'uns will be in to see him." To the thieves he said, "Let's get going."

Sir went with the constable, Mrs. Glynn, and the man in handcuffs. Meg watched closely. She saw the actress look back at Thunder in the tree.

When the constable drove Bill Purdy's car away, Meg ran to the tree where Thunder sat on a limb. In her sweetest Virginia drawl, she coaxed, "Come, Thunder. Come."

Thunder crossed his blue eyes at Kerry and Mike. He grumbled and scratched the collar he hated. The he slid headfirst down the tree trunk.

Meg picked up Thunder. She buried her face in his smooth fur. "I missed you, Thunder," she said softly.

"Cissie must have taken good care of him," Mike said. "He looks all right to me. But I don't see why everyone chased him. He's just a cat."

"He's not *just* a cat!" Meg said hotly. She hugged Thunder so tightly he kicked. Suddenly Meg smiled. She cried, "Kerry! Thunder was outside, not inside, when the man stood in the flower bed and watched us. Thunder was in the room with us when the man tried to break in."

"So?" Kerry asked, looking puzzled.

"And he was rambling while Mrs. Glynn asked

all the questions and searched Mrs. Partlow's garden. Thunder must have something Mrs. Glynn and Bill Purdy want."

"They want diamonds," Mike said. His eyes began to shine. He had found his "big story."

"Then Thunder has diamonds," Meg said. Tingling with excitement, she wiggled her fingers at Mike. "Loan me your knife, please, Mike."

"Sure," Mike said, reaching in his pocket.

"All Thunder has is a collar. That's in plain sight," Kerry said.

"So were the rest of the diamonds," Meg reminded them. She sat on the ground with her cat in her lap. She unbuckled Thunder's collar.

With Mike's knife, Meg pried open one of the metal bells. Out rolled a stone. A little bell clapper swung free with a musical tinkle.

"I *knew* it should sound like a bell," Meg said. "I *knew* I'd heard it." She rolled the stone in her palm.

"A diamond?" Kerry asked.

Meg nodded and shook the collar. "I'll bet they're

all here. No wonder Mrs. Glynn worried about my cat."

Meg stood up and lifted Thunder to her shoulder. She said, "I'll take these to Mrs. Partlow, quick, before they disappear. Just wait till I tell my dad—"

Meg clapped a hand over her mouth. "Oh!" she wailed. "Dad told me not to chase criminals."

Kerry giggled and hugged Meg. "You didn't. You chased Cissie and Thunder and three trained dogs."

"The dogs!" Meg and Kerry said at the same time.

Mike started up the slope. He said, "I'll bring in the poodles before Cissie decides to hide them under the bridge."

"Wait for me, Mike," Kerry said. "I want to tell Chappie good night. I've been neglecting him."

With the collar in her pocket and the one loose diamond in her hand, Meg settled Thunder on her shoulder. She started down Old Bridge Road.

The sun was almost down. Long shadows stretched from oaks, willows, and the hedge around Mrs. Partlow's garden. No car was hidden in the

A MEG Mystery

shadows. No animals pranced around wearing a fortune in stolen diamonds.

A man ambled around the curve where Culper Road and Upland Way joined the Old Bridge Road.

"Meg?" Mr. Wilson called. "It's getting dark. The missus worried about you. Thought I'd walk you home." As he came nearer he said, "See you found the tiger."

"Yes, Mr. Wilson," Meg said happily. "And you were right. Thunder was 'fixing to make mincemeat' out of that man who was in our house."

"I know. I was in the yard when the constable passed the house. He gave me the news."

Meg grinned. Nothing was secret in Hidden Springs.

"What's for supper?" Meg asked. "Thunder and I are hungry!"